9/09

Barbara Joosse

illustrated by Jan Jutte

Philomel Books

For Scott Treimel,
agent, friend, bad cop, hero and Bear.   —BJ

To all the brave kids in the world.   —JJ

One dark and snarly night
when Papa was away,
and Liam was a-snuggled in,
he heard the forest *crack* and
snap!
His heart thumped, *Danger!*

What could Liam do? He was just a boy (*thump thump*),
too small to fight off forest things.
He thought and thought a little more,

and suddenly he knew:
"I'll build a fort,
put in provisions—
sticks and string and double-cake—
then growl a warning . . .

ROAWR!"

Mama shook her finger.
"Use your inside voice!
No sticks in here! And no
double-cake!"

The forest grew deeper dark, the night grew long,
the clock *tick-tocked* to bedtime.
Mama tucked in Liam tight
and kissed him on the cheek good night.
He rubbed it off.

Mama opened windows wide,
turned off the lights, crawled into bed
and drifted off to sleep.

Tick-tock, the clock.
Snip-snap, the cracks.

Then . . .

ROAWR!

Liam rushed to Mama, called her name,
but she was snore asleep.

Oh no! Mama was delicious
to forest things, and he was just a boy (*thump thump*).
What could Liam do?

He thought and thought a little more,
and suddenly he knew:
"I'll pack my shovel, sticks and string
and double-cake,
then creep along on furry feet,
eyes sharp for . . ."

ROAWR!

There!
Bear clacked his teeth,
raised his snout and sniffed for sleeping Mama.

What could Liam do? He was just a boy (*thump thump*).
He thought for just a little bit and suddenly he knew:

"I'll dig a hole, spread sticks on top
and tie a string
to a bell on my windowsill."

Liam scarcely breathed.
He waited,
waited,
waited for the bell to . . .

RING!

Bear!

He rumbled in the hole,
slashed moonlight bloody with his claws
and bellowed . . .

ROAWR!

Now what?

Liam shivered. He was just a boy (*thump thump*).
But Bear was too big, too strong and fine
to stay inside a hole forever.
And out, Bear would eat up Mama!

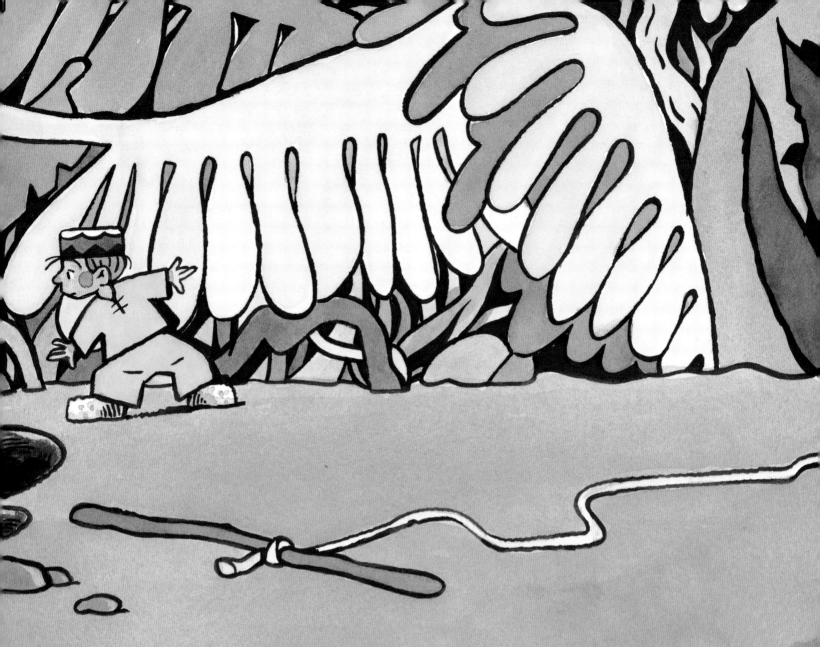

Liam thought and thought,
and suddenly he knew:
"Bear ate the cake, no lick of frosting left.
He's hungry!

"So I, a boy, a clever boy,
will search the woods,
the up and down,
the all around,
to find . . .

food for Bear! A bush!

Sweet berries,
ripe and red!"
Liam clawed them
off the branches,
gobbled some and
took the rest . . .

to Bear, who gulped them down.

ROAWR!

Now what?

Liam thought, but not for long (*thump thump*).

Then Liam knew:

"A bear so big and fine needs *more*."

So Liam wove a basket,
stuffed it full,
and dragged it back to . . .
Bear, who ate the berries up.

Roawr!

"More?"

A boy (*thump thump*), a clever boy,
knows this about a bear:
"A bear needs fish to eat."

Liam tied his string to a stick,
hooked a worm to a thorn,
and cast into the deep-down lake.

He snared a silver fish,
delicious to a bear.
Bear smacked his lips
and snatched the fish, *gulp.*

Ahhhh. Belly full, his ears flopped soft,
Bear curled into a ball to snooze,
zzzzzzzzzzz.

Now what? Now what do boys
so clever, brave and true,
with hearts a-thump for bears so fine
and Mamas sleeping in the night . . .
what do they do?

Liam knew:
"Bear *was* hungry, now he's *not*.
Mama will be safe.
I'll fix a way for Bear to climb
out, to be a bear.

And I . . . ?
A boy so brave and true—
am tired, too."

Now back at home,
Liam slippered off his furry
feet, and curled
into his cave to sleep.
Zzzzzzzzz.

Jan Jutte's work on *ROAWR!* was supported by a grant
from the Netherlands Foundation for Visual Arts,
Design and Architecture.

Patricia Lee Gauch, Editor

PHILOMEL BOOKS
A division of Penguin Young Readers Group.
Published by The Penguin Group.
Penguin Group (USA) Inc., 375 Hudson Street, New York, NY 10014, U.S.A.
Penguin Group (Canada), 90 Eglinton Avenue East, Suite 700, Toronto, Ontario M4P 2Y3, Canada (a division of Pearson Penguin Canada Inc.).
Penguin Books Ltd, 80 Strand, London WC2R 0RL, England.
Penguin Ireland, 25 St. Stephen's Green, Dublin 2, Ireland (a division of Penguin Books Ltd).
Penguin Group (Australia), 250 Camberwell Road, Camberwell, Victoria 3124, Australia (a division of Pearson Australia Group Pty Ltd).
Penguin Books India Pvt Ltd, 11 Community Centre, Panchsheel Park, New Delhi - 110 017, India.
Penguin Group (NZ), 67 Apollo Drive, Rosedale, North Shore 0632, New Zealand (a division of Pearson New Zealand Ltd).
Penguin Books (South Africa) (Pty) Ltd, 24 Sturdee Avenue, Rosebank, Johannesburg 2196, South Africa.
Penguin Books Ltd, Registered Offices: 80 Strand, London WC2R 0RL, England.

Design by Semadar Megged.   Text set in 19-point Triplex Serif Bold.
The illustrations were created in ink, watercolor and acrylic.

Library of Congress Cataloging-in-Publication Data
Joosse, Barbara M.   Roawr! / Barbara Joosse ; illustrated by Jan Jutte.   p. cm.   Summary: When Liam hears a loud roar in the middle
of the night, he must use all his ingenuity to protect his sleeping mother from a hungry bear.
[1. Bears—Fiction. 2. Self-reliance—Fiction.] I. Jutte, Jan, ill. II. Title.   PZ7.J7435Ro 2009   [E]—dc22   2008016907
ISBN 978-0-399-24777-4
1 3 5 7 9 10 8 6 4 2